PRAI

MW01015496

Top 10 Romance of 2012, 2015, and 2016.

— BOOKLIST: THE NIGHT IS MINE, HOT
POINT, HEART STRIKE

One of our favorite authors.

— RT BOOK REVIEWS

Buchman has catapulted his way to the top tier of
my favorite authors.

— FRESH FICTION

A favorite author of mine. I'll read anything that
carries his name, no questions asked. Meet your
new favorite author!

— THE SASSY BOOKSTER, FLASH OF
FIRE

M.L. Buchman is guaranteed to get me lost in a
good story.

— THE READING CAFE, WAY OF THE
WARRIOR: NSDQ

I love Buchman's writing. His vivid descriptions bring everything to life in an unforgettable way.

#2   2-14-18

FOR ALL THEIR DAYS

AN OREGON FIREBIRDS ROMANCE

M. L. BUCHMAN

Buchman Bookworks

SIGN UP FOR M. L. BUCHMAN'S
NEWSLETTER TODAY

and receive:
Release News
Free Short Stories
a Free book

Do it today. Do it now.
http://free-book.mlbuchman.com

Other works by M. L. Buchman:

"*M*oon eyes," Stacy whispered.

"I tell you what I'm gonna do," Maggie didn't even bother turning around. "This *chiquita* is going to poke out the eyes of those two *niños pequeños* and feed them to the pigeons." Being a Latina woman from Astoria, Oregon meant she didn't pull out her Spanish very often, but these *little boys* were getting irritating.

"Too bad there aren't any pigeons around here."

"Why you gotta spoil a girl's fun, huh? Just because you got Curt to put that pretty ring on your finger?" Maggie traded a grin with the Firebirds' Number One pilot.

"Yep. Must be why I do it." Stacy's voice went all dreamy in a way that no man was ever going to hear from Maggie Torres' lips.

She dug around in her toolbox until she found a nice thirty-inch long crowbar, nearly half as long as she was. "They still there?"

Stacy made a show of moving to check something in the MD 520N helicopter's cockpit, not that anything there mattered until Maggie finished servicing the engine.

"Uh-huh. About ten feet off your six."

It was cracking ninety today in the southwest corner of Oregon at the Illinois Valley Airport and the midday heat had her stripped down to a tank top and gym shorts while she worked. So of course the guys were watching the show when they were supposed to be cleaning out the trucks from the last wildland firefight.

She raised the crowbar as if to tap something on the engine that was out of her reach. Then she spun and swung her arm down. The eight pounds of steel spun through the air for one full turn, then spiked down to punch a hole in the dirt between Amos' and Drew's sneakers—which were maybe a foot apart. Both pilots yelped and scattered.

The bright flush on their cheeks as they went back to work told her they weren't even aware of staring. Two nice boys stuck in the middle of nowhere caught daydreaming about pretty women. Well, she didn't want no "nice" boy. She wanted someone who fired her blood like the inlet temperature of the 520N's Rolls-Royce 250 turboshaft engine—eighteen hundred degrees of pure heat.

"They're never going to stop, Maggie. They don't even know they're doing it," Stacy confirmed Maggie's own assessment as she yanked the crowbar out of the dirt, stalked back, and dropped it into the toolbox. "You're the prettiest woman for probably ten miles around. You make men's brains switch off."

"We're in the middle of the Siskiyou Mountains, probably a hundred miles."

"Two hundred," Stacy agreed.

"Now that might be bragging. Besides, I remember seeing *some* girl in a wedding dress recently who looked pretty damn hot."

"I did, didn't I? Killer dress you helped me pick out. Curt certainly seemed to think so."

"The man couldn't even speak," Maggie remembered his stunned puppy look. Maybe on the right man, Maggie wouldn't mind that look so much.

"Might not have spoken much, but he had plenty to 'say' when he took it off me."

It was one of the best parts of working for the Firebirds. Maggie loved the six machines she'd been hired to take care of. Loved watching the team of MD 520Ns fly to the firefight. But she also was getting seriously used to having a girlfriend in the outfit. She knew how she looked and that it had a way of pushing other women away.

Not Stacy. They'd hit it off early and solid, like a well-tuned V8 engine.

Jana Williams, the outfit's co-owner with Stacy's new husband was a little daunting, but she'd been that way when they'd both been in the Army. She and Jana hadn't overlapped much, mechanic and pilot, but Jana had given her such a sweet offer that she'd signed on with the Firebirds rather than another tour with the Army. While it might not be deep friendship, it counted for a whole lot.

Amos and Drew, however, were being a major pain in her ass—almost literally. She'd seen it the moment they crawled out of their matching black GTOs with red flames painted down the sides at the start of the season. They weren't bad guys. They just turned into moon-eyed stunned puppies whenever they got around her.

She snatched up a 12mm wrench and began checking the tightness of all of the hydraulic fittings while Stacy inspected the air filters, using compressed air to blow out any built-up fire ash. There were some tasks Maggie would let a pilot do, mainly because there was no way for them to screw it up.

"I want my man to be made of stuff better than…man."

"I don't know," Stacy moved on to checking the control linkages from the cyclic and collective controls to the rotor head.

Maggie had already done those, so it was a safe task. She wouldn't have let Stacy even do things like that, except she really *was* a good mechanic by anyone else's standards other than Papa or Maggie herself. Her father had serviced Coast Guard helos for thirty years; he still did. He'd started teaching her how to wrench a helo before she'd started kindergarten. Two tours in the Army, she'd had to put up with a ton of exactly the kind of shit Amos and Drew were doing. Two "macho" guys who couldn't figure out how to even speak to her.

"I like the stuff that Curt is made of," Stacy was doing more of that dreamy thing.

"That's 'cause you just got married, bitch, and like showing off. You don't got to be fishing around in the barrel like the rest of us poor *chicas.*"

"Nope," Stacy sounded far too happy about that fact.

But Maggie couldn't think of what to say back. Stacy was an awesome pilot, even Jana said so which meant something serious. She was totally nice, like girl-next-door nice. Maggie had always liked her three sisters, but they'd stab you in the back and steal your boyfriend faster than you could change your shoes if you let them. Stacy wasn't like that. She also was walking as if her feet weren't going to ever touch the ground again, which was just showing off to Maggie's way of thinking.

She sighed. Except for occasional fishing trips to the couple of bars in Cave Junction, it was going to be a long, dry summer. On the fire line, the firefighters usually just collapsed into exhaustion when they came off the line—not as if she had spare time and energy during a big fire herself.

Hydraulics were all tight. She began greasing the linkages to the rotorhead and NOTAR fan.

2

"*Heading* up," Curt called over the radio on the Firebirds' private frequency. The fire commander's frequency was set to just monitor.

"Roger that." Palo waited until Curt was aloft and far enough clear for the air turbulence to settle, before easing up on his own MD 520N's collective. With a full load of two hundred gallons of water aboard, he'd take the clearest air he could find to get lift.

There were just three of them fighting a small fire in the hills southeast of Depoe Bay along the Oregon Coast. He'd never imagined this section of the Oregon forest could *get* dry enough to burn. Some idiot hikers' campfire, sparking off after they were long gone because they didn't know how to douse it properly. It gave them work, he supposed. Department of Forestry would normally let something like this burn quietly to clear out the undergrowth, but the wind was sliding out of the northwest for a change and driving it toward the town of Siletz.

Not big enough to call out the full flight of six helos,

they'd loaded up just three of the six Firebirds and headed over to kill it off before it got out of hand.

Jasper followed him aloft as silently as ever.

There weren't any natural firebreaks between Depoe Bay and Siletz, but a team of hotshots were on the ground making one out of an old logging road. The Firebirds' assignment was to narrow the fire's head until it dead-centered on the break the hotshot crew was cutting. Then they'd hit any spot fires that cropped up once it got there. No reason to call in the big outfits yet, most of whom were fighting a blaze up north in the Columbia Gorge.

"How'd you do it, Curt?" The three of them flew in a line over the Black, as the burned-over section of a forest fire was called.

"I just fly low and hit the little button that says Tank Release on it when I'm over the flames."

"Ha. Ha. No. How did you get Stacy?"

"'Cause I'm just that good."

"Blind luck," Jasper commented drily as the three of them came up on the fire.

"Truth?" Palo eased in close behind Curt. A glance showed Jasper nowhere to be seen, which meant he was exactly astern. It was becoming the Firebirds' trademark: fly in fast and low in a tight line. Between them, they could lay six hundred gallons—a ton-and-a-half of water—in a tightly-connected clean line or a triple-layered inundation, dead on target. With a nearby water source, they could do it once every two minutes.

"Truth?" Curt left it hanging out there as he dove on the fire and Palo followed him down. They were coming in along the edge of a forested ridge. It was covered in hundred-foot Doug fir and trash alder. If they could keep the flames on the south side of the ridge, the fire would narrow itself as it burned along the sharpening valley which climbed up into the Coast Range.

"Truth is he has no idea," Jasper spoke up. Curt and Jasper went all the way back to grade school, which meant Jasper knew.

Curt sighed his agreement as he released his load over the edge of the fire. "If you really want to know, Palo, you need to ask Stacy. I have no idea what a woman that amazing sees in me."

That wasn't going to happen. If he asked Stacy, she'd want to know why. And if he told her *that*, she'd tell— Wasn't going down that way one bit.

Palo followed Curt's line, then peeled off to tank up. The Siletz River was close by, but it was too narrow with tall trees on both banks for most helos. Their little MD 520Ns could slip right in, lower a fifteen-foot long snorkel to suck up a load, and be on the move twenty seconds later without ever landing. What they didn't have in load-carrying capability—the big Firehawks could carry a thousand gallons to his two hundred—they more than made up in speed and agility.

Speed and agility? How in the world was that supposed to help him with a pixie-tall, Latina-fireball of a woman like Maggie Torres?

3

To Maggie, the campfire felt empty that night with just the three women around it.

Amos and Drew had gone into Cave Junction. Two thousand people made it the biggest town for thirty miles in any direction. Two thousand people, four restaurants, and very few bars made the odds of running into them far too likely. Besides, as much as Maggie liked men, that whole scene was getting old really fast.

Over the first couple months of the fire season, she'd already tried out most of the local boys. Very few even made it past the first-drink test.

It was a simple test. Could they share one drink without some remark that was the moral equivalent of the Jimmy Buffet classic, *Why don't we get drunk and screw.*

Even fewer had made it past the second-drink test: would her head hurt more if she finished the second drink, which she never actually did, or if she woke up beside the contender?

And the tourists who hit Cave Junction to visit the Oregon Caves—because no one else in their right minds except a wildland firefighter came out here—were traveling as couples. The Caves weren't really a single guy kind of attraction.

She, Stacy, and Jana didn't even have to change positions with the vagaries of the evening breeze—because there wasn't one. It was so quiet that the smoke rose straight up with only the occasional flicker of sparks. They just sipped their beers and watched the fire and the stars.

At least Amos and Drew—when their brains weren't switching off on them unexpectedly—were good for a laugh, bantering back and forth like twin brothers despite one being black and the other white. Maybe it was a New York City thing.

She was more of an Astoria, Oregon gal. Most of her childhood had been spent at the US Coast Guard Air Station. Sometimes she'd travel with Papa to Cape Disappointment on the Washington State side of the Columbia.

Cape Disappointment: another one of her life's ironies. The major Coast Guard installation in the Pacific Northwest perched close by the mouth of the Columbia River. It had some of the most dangerous waters in the entire country. Some said that there were more wrecks crossing the Columbia Bar than the entire Gulf of Alaska. All three of her sisters had married Coasties, but for her there had only been disappointment. Not a single one of them had been made of the same metal as Papa. Most Coasties wouldn't even give her the time of day once they learned she was Chief Torres' daughter. Her sisters never had that problem, so why did she?

So here they were, three women staring at the warm coals and flickering sparks. The former Siskiyou Smokejumpers Base had been closed in 1981 after launching over fifteen hundred fire jumps. She could feel the men who had lived here through the years—and not just because of the small museum and historic landmark buildings. It was in the night air. In the smell of dry pine and drier grass.

"Story time," Stacy broke the long silence.

Jana's grunt said she wasn't adverse to the idea, as long as it didn't start with her. She sat far enough back in her folding chair so that only her blonde hair and the steel hooks that had replaced her right hand showed. She could still fly like a demon, but she couldn't fly to fire because she couldn't work the thumb and finger controls on the cyclic. She was their head trainer and ran the business with an iron, or rather a *steel* hand, while her brother flew.

"I know you're both sick of me babbling about being married—"

"Totally," Maggie teased her.

"—so I'll shut up about that for a change. That leaves you, Maggie."

"Oh." That hadn't gone well. She listened to the night and could imagine the ghosts of shouts to "saddle up" over the racket of Pratt & Whitney Twin Wasp radial engines coughing to life on the DC-3 jump planes. It left a silence now broken only by the crackling fire and the occasional flutter of bat wings.

Story time had become something of a tradition among the women of the Firebirds. Ever since the massive misunderstanding that almost had Stacy leaving the outfit, they'd held story time. By telling each other pieces of their past when the guys weren't around maybe they could avoid messing each other up in the future. There weren't many opportunities, but they were slowly getting to know one another better for it.

"When Papa had to work late, I used to ride my bike over to the Astoria, Oregon Airport after dinner. I'd help

M. L. BUCHMAN

him service the helos, handing him tools and asking a
thousand questions. Afterward we'd sit out like this and
watch the stars. Sometimes we'd go across the runways to
sit beside the Columbia River and watch the ships come in
as the sun set over the Pacific."

"What did you talk about?"

"Not much. Engine mods maybe. Boy trouble, a little.
Let's just say that I started looking like this pretty early.
Having a *papaíto* who was a USCG mechanic and a chief
petty officer helped a lot with that."

"Was he pretty like you?" Jana tried to make it sound
as if she might be tempted.

"No. I'm a throwback. The shortest one in the family
by eight inches. Just like Nana—my grandmother. Ma's
pretty, but not in Nana's league, and all my sisters take
after Ma, kinda mostly. Papa is really solid, like a rock. Like
Palo I suppose." There was a parallel she'd never thought
of. "What is he anyway?"

"A hunk," Stacy was still so newly married that she saw
all men as beautiful, wonderful creatures.

Jana snorted and tossed her empty beer bottle toward
the small cooler.

At least she and Jana knew it was never that simple.

Maggie waved at the cooler to see if she wanted
another, but Jana shook her head in a shimmer of blonde
hair.

"You're going to laugh when I tell you what he really
is," Jana spoke little louder than the fire. "Palo Akana is
Finnish-Hawaiian. Though I don't remember which of his
parents is which."

"Last name Hawaiian, probably his dad," Maggie
figured.

"Hunk," Stacy affirmed.

Palo was so quiet that Maggie had never given him

much thought. Not awkwardly silent like Jasper—who only crawled out of his shell at all when…Jana wasn't around. Huh! That was interesting.

Palo wasn't Hawaiian large, but neither was he Finnish light. He was dark, handsome, and built rock-solid. He also flew so well that Jana and Curt had hired him, which said a lot about the man. Said a lot about Drew and Amos too—at least their abilities if not their shining personalities.

As if hearing her thoughts, there was the low thrum of a pair of diesel trucks coming along the Redwood Highway. She listened. V8. The deep note of a GMC 6.6 liter under moderate load. Enough tire noise to tell her there was a lot of rubber on the coarse-sealed road: like two pickups with rear dualies and hauling trailers.

"The boys are back."

"What?" Stacy lit up like…a newlywed. The girl couldn't help rubbing it in.

Jana was still twisting back and forth as if seeking the sound, not locating it until they were almost in the parking lot. Probably lost some sensitivity in all those years she'd flown for the US Army's 101st Airborne. Maggie missed those days herself sometimes, but she'd left voluntarily—unlike Jana after an accident took her hand.

With the hard crunch of gravel, the two GMC Denali pickups rolled in, each hauling a gooseneck trailer that had their helos tied onto the decks. They rolled up close to the fire before shutting down and clambering out.

"We killed that sucker!" Curt announced in a loud voice. "This boy needs a beer and a kiss."

"Not in *that* order you don't," Stacy leapt into his arms and Curt looked pretty damn pleased with the change of priorities.

Jasper crossed to the cooler and grabbed a pair of cold ones. He uncapped and tucked one in Curt's hand where it was still wrapped around his wife's back. Then he retreated to the shadows near Maggie—directly *opposite* Jana she noticed. He pulled down his white cowboy hat low enough to hide his eyes, but she'd wager he could still see across the fire just fine. Suspicions ninety percent confirmed.

Did Jana know? Not much got by her, but she wasn't looking toward Jasper either. So maybe not.

Ty, their summertime hired help who'd been off with the guys on the Siletz fire, headed off to get the fuel truck. She really needed to talk to him about relaxing at least *once* in a while. Nah, he was young. He'd learn it on his own. Besides, she was the last person who should teach anyone about relaxing.

Then Palo stepped around the back of the trailers, as if he'd circled to make sure everything had survived the five-hour drive back from the fire site. Or maybe so that she wouldn't notice him. He was like that—all stealth in plain view.

Maggie felt more than the fire's heat flash into her as she noticed where his eyes went. They didn't travel to Curt and Stacy still making a happy spectacle of themselves. They didn't go to Jana as she heckled her brother and sister-in-law. He stood back in the dark, but even by the fading reach of the firelight, she could see that he was looking directly at her.

And it wasn't the way that Amos and Drew did, staring in wonder.

He looked at her like a man fresh saved by a Coastie ocean rescue. The moment he stepped once more onto dry land—as if he'd never thought he'd see it again.

She tried to look away. Wanted to join in on Jana's razzing, though her throat was too dry and she couldn't seem to raise her beer.

Palo didn't flinch aside. She'd bet she could heave an

entire rack of crowbars into the ground between his feet and he'd just look down at them, and back up at her.

Having been caught staring, he didn't look away.

And until he looked away, she wasn't going to either.

But he didn't!

How had a girl from Astoria, Oregon ended up in a Mexican standoff with a Finnish-Hawaiian fire pilot?

And what was she going to do about it?

4

*P*alo waited. Waited to come to his senses. Waited for Maggie to blink so that he could convince himself that it wasn't him she was looking at. She never had before except in passing.

Not that he'd done anything to encourage it.

Men like him didn't deserve women like Maggie Torres. It wasn't just her looks. Five-foot-two of curvy Latina with dark brown hair down to her shoulder blades, so thick a man could get lost in it.

She was everything he wasn't.

Smart, funny, and a crazy good mechanic. People lit up the moment she entered a room and sighed sadly when she left them behind. Her easy laugh always brightened any gathering. She always had the quick joke or tease. By the time he thought one up, the conversation had long since moved on.

People barely noticed when he arrived or departed and he was fine with that. He preferred the quiet.

She had quiet moments too, though they were rare. She went silent when she was chasing a mechanical problem, focusing all that skill. But that wasn't it. It was the moment before she'd spotted him, while he was still on the far side of the trailers looking at her through the steelwork of the helos' landing skids.

Quiet. At peace. That's when her true beauty came out and shone brightest for him.

Definitely not the kind of quiet she was at the moment.

She looked across the sparks and darkness like a toreador throwing down the red cape in front of the bull, daring him to make the next move. He could feel the impact of those dark eyes aiming bolts of fire in his direction until he was surprised that the gravel didn't turn to lava all around him.

What would it be like to be with a woman like that? To take her down and hold her close?

Not for him. Not for the kid from the San Francisco streets.

His gang had chosen his first name. "I'm gon' be rich someday! You just see," he'd declared in his five-year old surety. "Rich? You must be from Palo Alto. That's where those rich folk live. We gon' call you Palo." He'd chosen Akana because, when child services grabbed him after he was caught robbing a grocery store at eight, it had sounded cool and Japanese. And Japanese were all smart, rich, and drove BMWs. Instead, he'd been fostered to a guy who drove a rattletrap Ford pickup and flew helicopters for the power company—traveling the high-power lines year in and year out looking for problems. Palo had flown with him whenever he could so that he didn't have to see the string of men his foster mom entertained whenever her husband was gone.

Palo hadn't been along when the helo failed high in the Sierra Nevada. They'd traced it back to the mechanic—a mechanic who lived nowhere close to Maggie Torres' standards. They'd fired the mechanic, hired a new one, bought another bird, and hired Palo to take his foster father's place. He'd flown those same lines for six years before Curt Williams had hired him away.

It had been years before he looked up his own name and decided he was Finnish-Hawaiian to the rest of the world. It was certainly better than whoever he really was and he'd decided to keep the name.

And all he could do was stare across the fire at the most beautiful and amazing woman he'd ever seen and know for a fact that he had no right whatsoever to cross one step closer.

So instead, he nodded to her briefly and turned back into the night.

There he could at least dream that he was more than he was.

5

"What's with you?" Jana called out.

Maggie blinked over at her after Palo faded back into the darkness from which he'd so briefly emerged.

Jana twisted around to look over her shoulder, but there was nothing to see.

Again she asked her question.

"I'm not sure," was the best answer Maggie could find. Why would a man like Palo concede defeat like that? He'd looked beaten before he nodded to her and turned away. "I'm not sure…" But she rose to her feet and had to veer sharply after three steps so that she didn't walk straight into the fire.

"What's with her?" Jana asked no one in particular.

If anyone answered, Maggie didn't hear them.

Palo hadn't gone far. He sat on the tail of the second trailer. It was a low-bed, so he sat with his feet on the dirt, looking up at the stars. This far away the campfire offered only the vaguest silhouette. There was no moon yet and her eyes were only slowly adapting to starlight.

"Hey, Akana," she tried to keep it light.

"Hey, Torres." Palo's tone did remind her of Papa's. It simply said, *yep, here I am.* Hard to read what he was thinking one way or the other.

"Mind if I sit?"

"Help yourself." No shrug, that she could see. No hint of anything, except that she should help herself.

So, she scooted up on the trailer's deck, ending up a little closer to him than she intended, but didn't want to move away either. She knew that not everyone shared her ideas about close personal space. Actually, that was another thing that reminded her of Papa…he was the only one she'd really enjoyed having a closer personal space with. Despite that, she didn't feel any pressure to move away from Palo.

She swung her feet above the dirt for something to do.

"What was that?"

Palo didn't play dumb, which she liked. Instead, she could make out that he was staring at the stars.

So, for a while, she stared with him and watched Orion the hunter and Taurus the bull fighting the battle that they'd been having since the Greeks had named the constellations a kagillion years ago.

"There's a lot to admire about you, Torres," Palo said to the darkness as if it was plain fact.

"It's skin deep, Akana."

"I get that. Not what I was talking about. The way you're put together gets a man's attention, no question about that. It's what's past that I was talking about."

Maggie tried to catch her breath. No one admired her like that since… No. It was time to stop drawing parallels between her Papa and any man she was interested in. It wasn't fair to the man. If she kept comparing Palo to Papa, she'd never see the man as clearly as Stacy saw Curt—loving him with all of his shortcomings. If he—

Holy Mother! She had not just thought about being interested in Palo Akana.

But the idea, now that she'd thought of it, didn't sound as crazy as she expected it to.

Palo still sat. It was a comfortable silence, one that wasn't pushing all of her action buttons. It was the kind of silence that invited questions into it.

But she didn't know where to start.

"Finnish-Hawaiian, huh? What was that like?"

Palo was silent so long that she wondered if she'd somehow misunderstood something.

Then he sighed. "Of all the places in the world, you had to start there?"

She didn't know what to say, so she stared at the sky and waited.

---

6

*T*alking about his past always wrung Palo dry. He wasn't sure the last time he'd been so exhausted. They'd fought fire for four straight days. They'd started this morning at sunrise and only been released at five o'clock. Everyone had agreed they wanted to get back to the Firebirds' base, so they'd driven through the evening and the slow mid-summer sunset to reach the Illinois Valley Airport.

To see the women there, sitting around the fire as if waiting for them, had caught him so off guard. Curt welcomed by Stacy like he was coming home. The crew sitting around the campfire like they all belonged. Palo had never belonged anywhere except for his early days in the gang and flying beside his foster father.

But none of that was what had knocked him back.

Now that he'd spilled his past in the dirt beneath Maggie Torres' feet, it felt as if all life had been ripped out of him. Nothing remained except for the scorched Black.

He'd only told bits and pieces of his past to anyone before, never the whole thing. It always earned him, "Oh you poor thing," or something like that as if he was a wounded puppy. It hadn't taken him long to learn to keep his mouth shut. Why hadn't he been able to do that around Maggie Torres?

"I went back and looked up missing persons reports. You know, for kids lost around that time," apparently there was even more to dump at Maggie's feet. "You wouldn't believe how many kids every year, just in San Francisco. Almost two thousand: runaway, family abduction, unknowns…"

Still Maggie gave him her silence. He couldn't look down from the sky where his dreams lay to see her reaction. All he could hold onto was that she was still there beside him.

"I figure I belonged to the gang. They were my first memories anyway. A lot of teen pregnancies. Our gang leader would have been thirteen or so back then—could have been my dad, if he even knew. Moral standards and monogamy weren't real priorities when you're trying to survive on the streets. I tried to find them years later, but they'd disappeared into the dust. It was all Pinoy Pride and Nortenos the one time I went looking. Who knows what it is now? Haven't been back."

Maggie rested one of those fine, strong clean hands on his shoulder. They might be covered in grease or fire ash, but they were ever-so clean in other ways.

Here it came. *Poor little boy.* At least she wasn't disgusted and running away, but this wasn't much better. He hated pity.

"How did you become like you are?"

He looked down at her in surprise. The crescent moon had cracked over the Siskiyous while he'd told his tale. It now lit her eyes enough to see that there weren't tears there. Not pity at all. No way she could be impressed, but he didn't know what else to call her look.

"My foster dad. He was a good man. Ex-military pilot. Never spoke about it…or anything else. Real quiet type. Even more than me. Showed me by example what I always figured a man should be. My foster mom didn't set much of an example about women though."

"Where did you learn about them? What a woman *should* be?"

Palo dug down, but couldn't find the words. He'd always thought a woman was what he found in the bars. He'd seen others, women in couples and the like, but they were always at a distance. Somehow *other*.

He flew the lines, endless miles of power looping from one remote tower to the next. Every now and then finding a broken insulator and a dangling line. Other times finding where a tree had fallen and damaged a trestle tower. Illegal, and insanely dangerous, TV antennas rigged high in the steel. Three bodies of sport climbers who hadn't understood the random whimsical nature of the voltages they were messing with.

Coming "to land" only among the male mechanics and other pilots. Women for him spent their lives perched on bar stools. Buying them when he needed one: sometimes with dinner and drinks, sometimes with cold, hard cash.

He'd never thought of women as much else, until he'd seen Maggie Torres lift a wrench and tackle a helicopter like it was an old friend. Stacy and Jana were other examples, now that he thought about it.

But he'd only ever seen Maggie.

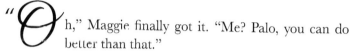

7

"Oh," Maggie finally got it. "Me? Palo, you can do better than that."

He just shook his head like a cornered bull.

"I'm like the least girlie girl on the planet. I was such a tomboy that I made Coast Guard jocks feel like sissies. I only put on a dress and flirt in the bars to prove to myself that I'm not a complete lost cause as a woman."

"You're *not* a lost cause," his voice was a low growl. The first emotion he'd revealed in the whole telling of his awful past and it was in the defense of *her* femininity. There was a laugh.

"Palo!" The frustration in her own voice earned her a smile. "No one in their right mind should be attracted to me."

"Everyone in their right mind *is* attracted to you."

"For all of the wrong reasons!" She didn't like that they all wanted her body, not her. But Palo had already listed why he was attracted to her. His reasons were all about her real self and not—well, only a little—about how she looked.

Palo waited her out.

"How come you never said anything? How many times did you sit in a bar and watch me…" Maggie couldn't even finish the sentence. …*flirting with useless men.*

"Don't go to the bars much anymore. Not since I met you."

And he was right. He always had some excuse or other to beg off except when all the Firebirds went as a team.

But Maggie pictured him there anyway. Pictured him sitting quietly at a stool down the end. It was easy to imagine him there—the strong silent type. Easy to imagine his foster dad beside him. She could hear the love, even if he dismissed it. *Two* strong, silent men. Sitting at the end of the bar, sipping their beers. One teaching the other what it meant to be a man just by his steadiness, by his commitment to his work.

And it was far too easy to imagine her not noticing him. Yet in her mind's eye, Palo made all those other boys pale by comparison. She could feel him watching her in her imagination until her entire body tingled for real.

"Palo."

"Uh-huh."

She dropped down on her feet and turned to stand between his knees.

"Palo."

He considered her for a long moment in silence, then his eyes went wide. "No, Torres. You deserve better than me."

"And you don't think that's for me to decide?"

He tried leaning back, but was stopped by the helo anchored to the trailer close behind him.

"Palo."

"Torres, don't!"

"You're not getting off that easy. You've got to at least

32

kiss me once. There is no way that a man can tell me I'm the model of all womanhood and not kiss me to prove his point."

Palo groaned as if in agony.

It was almost enough to make her step back. But she hesitated a moment too long.

He grabbed her and pulled her hard against him until her thighs were pressed against the flat metal edge of the trailer and her upper body was crushed against the wonderfully solid chest of his. Palo had been carved out of granite, fire-hot stone that scorched her fingers to touch as her hands came to rest there.

For all the violence of his embrace, his kiss hesitated half a breath away, then settled upon her lips with all the gentleness of the still night.

This, was all she could think. *This* was what she'd been looking for in all those bars and with all those men. Heat, power, tenderness—all fabricated of something that wasn't like any other man but remained fantastically male.

Maggie was so lost in the moment that all she could offer was a small choking cry of shock when Palo pulled back abruptly, forcing her to step away with his hands on her shoulders.

Before she could recover, he was gone into the dark.

The ground weaved beneath her like a storm-tossed rescue boat. Without Palo holding her, it felt as if the lightest breeze—the slightest impetus from a passing owl's wing—would take her to her knees.

"That," Stacy said from where she leaned in the darkness against the helicopter on the other trailer. "Is *exactly* what I've been talking about."

Maggie couldn't even nod.

8

*H*e shouldn't have just walked away. But he had to protect Maggie from himself. Palo knew only one use for women—up with the skirt, down with the underwear, and do that deed until they both were done.

That was the lesson he'd seen in the older members of the gang. It was the lesson his foster mom had certainly taught—even offering herself to him when he was man-grown. Instead he'd taken one of the high school cheerleaders for the football team as his first time. Couldn't even remember her first name—might not have ever known her last one.

It was the lesson that every woman in every bar had taught him.

Instead, the moment he'd touched Maggie, his world had shifted. He'd never taken his time kissing a woman. Hell, he'd screwed far more women than he'd ever kissed because that's what women were for.

With Maggie Torres, he'd wanted to give her a gentleness he'd never found—*never imagined*—before.

And she'd responded with an openness and an innocence that had shocked him to the core. Shocked them both apparently. That little cry as he'd stepped her back from the kiss told him more than he'd ever known about her.

Maggie was an innocent. Not a virgin—he wasn't dumb enough to think that, or care. Not unworldly either.

But she thought the world shone as a far nicer place than he knew it was.

A part of him had wanted to take her. Tear away her t-shirt to dig his fingers into those perfect, high breasts. Yank down her cute little gym shorts, bend her over, and ram himself home. He knew about that. He knew how to do that.

He knew nothing about how to kiss and hold a woman who sighed her breath into his mouth as he wrapped his arms around her. He'd filled his hands with her rich bounty of hair. Rather than an urge to yank down on it to force her head back—to ravage her neck and chest—he'd wanted to brush it over his face and feel how the soft curls touched lighter than fire smoke.

She had stood, shining in the moonlight, stunned into a small whimper. The violence of his desperate need for her was so close to the surface that she'd known. She must have.

He had wanted her so badly in that instant, that he could no longer trust himself. Another breath filled with her scent, another heartbeat racing because of the feel of her, and he was going to take her down like any bar whore.

Not Maggie.

So he'd slid clear and stalked away into the darkness not knowing where he was going. He'd finally slept under a tree, having to wait for dawn to figure out where he was and walk the five miles back to the airport.

Thank god he'd arrived just in time for another fire call. It spared him having to face her as they all raced to load up the remaining helos and start the five-hour drive down to Chico, California. A prairie fire was turning its sights on the airport there—with the town not far behind.

9

*A*s usual, she, Jana, and Ty drove the three pickup trucks, each towing a pair of MD 520N helicopters on long trailers. In her truck, Maggie had Stacy in the front and Jasper in the back. Curt and Palo rode with Jana and the knuckleheads ended up in Ty's truck.

It always ended up that way and for the first time, she was beginning to understand why. Even if she didn't like it.

She'd tried to maneuver Palo into riding with her and Stacy. Not so that they could talk, exactly. But maybe they'd be able to anyway if he sat up front and Stacy pretended to be asleep in the back.

But that would mean Jasper would have to ride with Jana. He made it clear that wasn't going to happen, by chucking his go-bag in the back seat of her own truck.

Instead it was her and Stacy, with Jasper catching some shut-eye.

"It was one kiss," she'd whispered to Stacy after they were finally away from Cave Junction. They'd all grabbed breakfast at the River Valley Restaurant. They'd pulled a couple tables together which the waitresses soon buried in tall stacks, waffles, and biscuit-and-gravy combos. Palo had somehow ended up at the opposite end of the long table.

"Uh-uh. Not pulling the wool over this gal's eyes. I *know* what a normal kiss looks like," Stacy sounded entirely too pleased with herself.

Maggie had to remember that she wasn't the dreamy airhead she'd been appearing to be lately. She was a top pilot with an amazing track record against fire. Other than Jana, she was probably the brains of this outfit.

"Is that what happened to him?" Jasper wasn't snoozing off his breakfast the way he'd appeared to be. "He never came back to the bunkhouse last night. Kissed you, huh? Explains what he was talking about."

"What he was talking about?" Maggie wasn't sure she wanted to know.

"Tell us! Tell us!" Stacy twisted around enough to look back, meaning there was no escape now.

"Was asking about how Curt got you, Stacy."

"What did he say?" Stacy went off into her dreamy world voice.

"You think he knows? He told Palo to ask you."

And Stacy sighed happily. "That's my Curt. Just like Jana warned me. The best of men, just not a real deep thinker."

"So how did he get you?" Jasper's tone changed and Maggie wished she could turn to see his expression. His ever-present cowboy hat made him impossible to read in the rearview mirror.

"Blind luck," Stacy sighed.

Jasper harrumphed. "Exactly what he said."

"It's true. He's just this great guy. I haven't had a lot of experience with those but he completely sold me on them. Who's on your horizon, Jasper?" She turned to Maggie when he didn't answer. "We need to find Jasper a girl."

"Not gonna happen," and she could see him pull his cowboy hat down even further, indicating he was done with this conversation. Maggie was sure that she knew the answer he was avoiding.

"Looks like you already found your man," Stacy bubbled happily, missing all of the dynamics.

There was no way that a kiss, one kiss, could mean that. She'd kissed plenty of men, but not one had been like Palo. It was like he was worshipping at the altar, so gentle and sweet that it had wholly taken her breath away. No one had ever kissed her like that before.

She could feel the need in him. Could feel its fire scorching her. Maggie had even felt the violence in him, the need to take so strong, yet held under such perfect control that he could hold her that lightly.

What would it be like to just let herself be taken? To give herself over to a man's desires when what he desired was her? Because he absolutely didn't see her as "just some woman." A man like him didn't need to control himself around "just some woman." He was good-looking, incredibly strong, and there wasn't any doubt in Maggie's mind about his ability to deliver anything a woman could want. She—

"You need a mirror," Stacy broke in on her thoughts as they rolled through Grant's Pass and picked up I-5 south.

"Why?"

"You know that look you keep accusing me of?"

"No!" Maggie definitely had *not* gone all dreamy on a guy after a single kiss.

Though it had been an *amazing* kiss.

10

"Not talkin' about that." Palo hunched down in the back seat and wished there was a way he could disappear. He'd already talked more with Maggie last night than he did in most weeks. He was talked out. He was done.

"Well, you did something to her, Palo," Jana was at the wheel, but had twisted the rearview mirror so that she was staring straight at him each time she glanced away from the road.

"I kissed her. That's all I did."

Curt turned to look back at him. "You kissed, Maggie Torres? You lucky shit."

"You're happily married, remember?" Jana reminded her brother.

"Didn't say it was me. Didn't say I was trying to," Curt backpedaled fast. "Just saying that Maggie lets very few men aboard. Damn, brother!" He held up a fist for Palo to do a fist bump with. He sighed and did it because he knew Curt wouldn't let it go until he had.

"Assholes," Jana grumbled as they twisted and turned

down the steep hills before hitting the open flatlands of Medford.

"Hey!" Curt had turned away, but now twisted back to look at him.

"No." It was too easy to guess where Curt's thoughts had gone and he didn't want him telling his sister. He didn't want it getting back to Maggie.

"That's why you were asking how I *caught* Stacy."

"Blind luck," Jana zinged him.

"Why does everyone keep saying that?" Curt faced forward and folded his arms over his chest.

"Think about how amazing Stacy is." Jana kept facing straight ahead, but Palo could feel her smiling.

"Yeah," Curt sighed. "Blind luck. You gotta do better, Palo. Don't let a woman like that slip through your fingers. We're talking about a major keeper."

A couple miles passed in silence, something Curt was never good at.

"Hey! We gotta get you a man, sis."

"Not in this lifetime," she held up the hooks that were her right hand. "Nobody sees me past these."

"Gotta be someone. Come on, Palo. Who do we know that deserves my sister?"

That was the problem.

Did he himself deserve a woman like Maggie Torres?

She *was* a major keeper. But was he?

11

"Enough already!" Maggie stood beside his door the moment Palo landed the helo.

She was wearing a wide-brimmed goofy white sun hat with her mechanics coveralls—which she'd hacked off as short shorts. The woman was so damn cute he couldn't stand it.

He was just in from the last run of their fifth day on the Chico fire. It was half an hour to sunset and the little MD 520Ns didn't have the expensive, and heavy, gear to be night-certified. Just as well, they needed eight hours rest out of every twenty-four and that's about all the darkness there was this time of year.

He was hot, sweaty, hungry, and tired.

He was hot for the little slip of a mechanic standing there with her fists propped on the toolbelt hanging slantwise on those ever-so nice hips. Getting sweaty with her sounded even better than a shower. He was hungry for the taste of her. And he was tired of running away.

"I'm a grown woman despite my size."

He wasn't going to argue that point.

"I know what I want."

"Fine," he grunted against a dry throat. Flying over the fire did that. Flying over one in the superheated flatlands of Chico, California could parch a man for life. The two together sucked.

"Fine?" Causing her to blink in surprise.

"Fine." More than fine. "Where and how soon?"

She pointed as imperiously as a queen in a toolbelt, coveralls, and fashionable sunhat could. It was summer and the campus was mostly empty. With the airport smoked out and shut down—though not burned yet—their six helos were lined up in two rows on the open field outside the stadium. The college had opened up one of the dorms for the firefighters.

The rooms were doubles with two small beds and zero sound insulation. He'd bedded enough coeds when he was that age to know. That would never do.

"Get in." When she started to protest, he pulled the door shut in her face.

She huffed around the nose of the helo as he wound the engine back to life. Her hair caught and fluttered in the vagaries of the air turbulence coming off the flattened blades. He pushed in a little bit of negative lift with the cyclic, sucking the air up through the main rotor. It made her hair float up off her shoulders as she clamped a hand atop her hat. Yes, he remembered her hair's lightness in his hands and couldn't wait to touch her again. Why he'd hidden from her for five days was…well, obvious. To be done with that was more relief than a cold shower could ever provide.

Once she'd shed her toolbelt and was buckled in, he took them aloft.

The other helos, which had been coming in behind him, hesitated when they saw the two of them together through the large windshield. Curt waggled his helo side to side in a cheery wave, as did Stacy. Jasper just flew by. Drew and Amos seemed to stumble in the air.

He was past caring what others thought.

Palo flew them up into the hills east of Chico. The hills climbed quickly in a jumble of eroded valley through the tall buttes. The Big Chico Creek had cut especially deeply and still flowed year-round. Its rollicking course had been turned into a nature park.

"The entrance to Bidwell Park is closed by the fire, they emptied the place out three days ago even though the park itself is safe."

He found the spot he was after and spiraled them down. A giant snag, an old tree long since shed of life and bark, stood tall and weather-whitened over a tiny meadow surrounded by towering fir and spruce. The twenty-seven foot sweep of the MD 520N's rotors was a tight squeeze into the small clearing, but it fit.

Along one edge of the clearing, shaded by a few trees, there was a large pool in the stream formed by a rise of boulders at one end. At the other end, a waterfall splashed loudly into the upper end of the pool.

Maggie had gone quiet and he didn't know what to think. He did the full shut down. Even when he opened the door to let in the cool of the evening, she didn't budge.

He circled around and opened her door.

She unbuckled, stepped down, and into his arms. No kiss, no hug. She simply tucked her hands under her chin and leaned in against his chest. He wrapped his arms around her and wondered if they could stay like this forever.

"Thank you."

"For what? I haven't done anything yet." Maggie

rubbed her face on his sweat-stained shirt as if she didn't care that he stank.

"For bringing me here. For letting this be important."

He gathered a handful of that luxurious hair and tugged it just enough to get her to look up at him.

"You *are* important."

She nodded once. Then again. "So are you. I'd have taken you either way. A fun tussle or this. But I wanted to thank you for this."

"That doesn't cut out the fun tussle part, does it?"

Her smile went electric. "Let's find out."

"*F*un tussle," Maggie managed on a half laugh.

Palo managed to grunt an amused agreement that vibrated down her length as she still lay upon his chest.

They lay on one of the helo's emergency blankets spread close beside the stream. They had splashed in wearing their clothes, because they needed washing as badly as their bodies. The clothes had soon been tossed on the bank, but they'd swum back and forth in the fifty-foot pool of Brown's Hole for a long time.

Rather than cooling her off, the delay as they'd floated and talked had given the banked fires time to rekindle and burn anew. Any doubts she had were scorched away when he touched her for the first time as the last ray of sunlight snaked up their canyon to light the pool. His rough hand, softened by the water, had brushed along the side of her breast like an invitation. One she hadn't refused.

Now, hours later, she could only lie atop him and listen to the night in wonder.

The first time, after she'd fished out some of the

protection she'd bought this morning, she had let him take and plunder, because the need was so great and burned so hot that it couldn't happen fast enough for her.

The second time, she had taken him. Spending the time to appreciate, to caress, and to feel. *Holy Mother, to feel!* Never had a man made her cry aloud with the pure joy of the moment...her voice had echoed off the basalt walls.

"No way we can keep this from the others. One look at our smiles will give us away." Now, at least, she knew where Stacy's outrageous grin came from.

"Can't keep a damned secret in this outfit anyway." Palo sounded grouchy about it.

"Like you talking to Curt about how he got Stacy?"

Palo groaned.

"So is that what you're looking for? Happy ever after?"

"What about you?" She almost called him on dodging the question, but she didn't know herself and had to think about it.

"Mama and Papa had a great relationship. Even with four girls running around with a thousand demands, they always found ways to be together. They'd hold hands while watching TV. Anything."

"Well? Do you want that?" Palo's voice was so gentle.

She wanted... "More."

"More than happy ever after?"

She hid her face against his chest—she'd never told anyone the last part.

"What?" Palo kissed her on top of the head as he flipped a blanket over them against the cooling evening. Sensing her silence, he asked again. "What is it, Torres?"

She couldn't ignore a voice like that, so concerned, so willing to listen. But she couldn't do it.

"I just want more. That's all."

She snuggled down once more on his glorious chest,

hiding and she knew it. She tucked her head under his chin. His breathing slowed, then his hands slipped off her back until he lay limp beneath her.

This?

She listened to him sleep in the darkness.

This she most *definitely* wanted. For as long as she could have it.

13

"*W*hat the hell, Palo?" Curt was right in his face and he couldn't do anything about it because Curt was absolutely right.

He'd screwed up...in flight! The Firebirds had labored long and hard to perfect tight formation flying in the chaotic air currents over a forest fire. Which meant that when he screwed up today, he'd nearly taken three other birds down with him. It was only by some piloting miracle, and a lucky updraft that any of them were still alive.

"Well?"

He could only shrug. He had no idea what had happened.

"You uncaring son of a bitch! You're grounded!" Curt stalked off.

The other pilots who'd gathered to listen—though Amos had still been so shaky that he'd sat on the ground—looked at him in silence a moment longer.

He shrugged again. It wasn't that he didn't care. It was that he didn't know what had happened. He'd never come so close to dying. And to take others out with him *was* unforgivable.

Grounded.

Exactly what he deserved. But what the hell was he supposed to do now?

A hand rested on his back. After a month of living with and making love to Maggie Torres, he knew that touch better than his own.

He couldn't turn to face her.

"I saw the video." All of the Firebirds had multiple cameras to record their successes. Now they had recorded his failure. "What happened?"

Since shrugging hadn't worked, Palo tried shaking his head.

"Don't you *dare* brush me off, Palo Akana!" He'd only roused Maggie's temper a few times over the last month, but she'd given him a deep and abiding respect for it.

"I'm not. I really don't know what happened."

With her lightning quick change, the woman who came around in front of him was all sympathy and worry, not anger.

"One moment we were flying clean. Then I lost a chunk of time. Seconds at most. But it was just a blank." Each word hurt to bring up, but to answer the fear in Maggie's eyes he forced himself to find them.

"Eleven seconds," she whispered. "You flew at a hundred and seventy miles an hour for eleven full seconds without a single course change—not even a wiggle in flight. Like you'd been hypnotized by that tree."

He remembered *that* tree. An old monster of the forest reached up almost three hundred feet. Every inch of it a roaring torch and he'd flown at it like a moth seeking the flame. He'd come to—eleven full seconds? Unthinkable!— less than a second from the tree. He'd slammed the cyclic sideways, cutting a hard turn, almost putting his rotor blades through Stacy's helo. She'd hauled back, letting him pass mere feet below her, but her action had Jasper and Drew nearly ramming her from behind. His own correction had been so hard that only a lucky updraft had kept him clear of the burning treetops—though it had almost cooked him alive.

That's when the shakes hit him.

Maggie wrapped her arms around him and held on. He didn't deserve it, but she did.

Grounded? He should be cashiered and have his license revoked.

"I really screwed up, Maggie." He leaned down far enough to bury his face in her hair. "I don't know why. I just don't…"

"Shh!" She stroked her hands down his back. "We'll figure it out. I believe in you. We'll solve this."

And that's when he remembered.

He knew exactly what had gone wrong up there. It wasn't *that tree* that had hypnotized him.

The truth was even worse than he'd feared.

Palo tried to push Maggie away. When it didn't work, he tried harder. When she finally let go, he was pushing her hard enough that she tumbled over backward, landing hard on her butt.

"Steer clear of me, Torres. Oh shit! Please just stay away."

His Pontiac Firebird was parked by the small hut he'd shared with Maggie whenever they'd been in camp over the last month, as if he deserved to have a place to call his own.

Keys in his pocket.

He climbed in and was headed out of the parking lot before Maggie was even back on her feet. He punched up through the gears until the Redwood Highway was a blur. Fifty twisting miles to the coast at Crescent City, California. Maybe he wouldn't stop. Just do everyone a favor and plow straight into the ocean and put himself out of everyone's misery.

Palo knew he wouldn't. He'd never once thought of suicide, not even listening to his foster mother grunt away for the third trick of the night on the other side of the thin bedroom wall. But there was a part of himself he'd kill if he could.

And it wasn't the part that had fallen in love with Maggie Torres.

14

"*K*eys! Now!"

Curt pulled them slowly out of his pocket with a puzzled expression on his face. Maggie grabbed them out of his hand and raced over to his classic Trans Am.

"Hey!" Curt shouted after her, but she ignored him. All she knew was that the man she loved had just driven away from her without explanation and that her Denali pickup wasn't up to catching Palo's Firebird.

She slammed out of the parking lot spraying a great fan of gravel. She was in second by the time she hit the road and the tires chirped hard on the pavement when they caught.

Hammering through the tiny hamlet of O'Brien, she spotted Carl on the road in his police cruiser. The speed limit for town was down to fifty, just as she was cracking ninety in fourth gear. He chirped his siren at her as she flew by, but the Firebirds all had black cars with red flames on them—except of course Curt's which had the red and gold Firebird on the hood. They were known and he let her go by. She saw his smile flash when they were just even and he chirped the siren again in greeting. Maggie would have to be extra nice to him next time.

After she caught and killed that Finnish-Hawaiian bastard street punk from San Francisco, Palo Akana.

She spotted his car just after the long straightaways of Oregon ended and they flashed across the California border. The narrow two-land road grew narrower and began twisting down a sharp canyon between densely forested hills. She kept her foot in it and would have to remember to tell Curt that his right front suspension needed to be tightened up and his carb was running a little lean—because damn this was a sweet ride and it should be treated right.

California CHIPS were notoriously less tolerant than Oregon's Staties. Thankfully, Palo wasn't pushing it, so she caught up fast.

She took him on a blind corner, then slammed on her brakes as she cut in front of him. He skidded into a four-wheel drift, leaving long black streaks on the pavement before he bounced into a dirt pullout high on a curve. Lucky for him she hadn't caught him on the other side of the curve or he'd be nose down in Griffin Creek right about now which sounded fine to her.

She thought about ramming him, but didn't want to ding the boss' pretty car. If she'd been in her Denali she have run right over the top of Palo's old Firebird.

"Who the hell taught you to drive, woman?"

"*Mi papa*, so don't go there!" She'd never been so mad in her life as she stormed up to him.

He leaned back against his car with folded arms over his chest and glowered down at her.

"And don't be trying that shit either, Akana. You do *not*

walk away from me. You can yell at me, cry on me, make love to me, but you do *not* walk away. Ever!"

Palo watched her for a long moment. Then he reached out a hand and it was all she could do to not flinch away as he brushed her cheek. "Never seen you cry, Maggie."

"I don't." *Ever!* But his finger was wet. She brushed at her cheeks and felt the hot water there. "I don't!" Insisting sounded stupid, but it was all she had.

"Okay," Palo shrugged and refolded his arms.

No point in hitting him, her fist would just bounce off. "Where's a crowbar when I need one?"

He crossed to his trunk, opened it and pulled out a car jack handle. He handed it to her.

"Do your worst." And he looked even sadder than she felt.

"You just don't walk away," she threw the jack handle into the dirt where it stuck point first and quivered. "Mama did that. I can't have that twice in my life."

He blinked, just once. Palo might not talk much, but he wasn't slow. "But you said…"

"After we were all grown and gone. One day she just—left. Her note to Papa said, 'Don't come looking for me.' That's all. Took her car, her clothes, and one half of the bank account. Nothing else. I mean nothing. Not photo albums, not a can of god forsaken soup. We never heard from her again. Just about killed Papa."

"Aw, shit, Torres. Okay, never walk away from you. Got it."

Struggling for air, refusing to give in to the sobs that wanted to follow the tears, she forced herself to look once more at Palo. Unable to speak, she could only wait.

"So why did I, huh?" He grunted to himself.

Maggie could only nod in response.

He looked up at the sky so long, that she too looked

aloft. Low alder and high Douglas fir. The two-lane road was deep in the valley cut by Griffin Creek. She could hear it bubbling away in the background. Above was a slice of blue. It was an Oregon blue, pure except for a dusting of sea mist, softening without stealing the beauty of the color.

"The only place my life has ever made sense was up in that sky. Flying with my foster dad. Working the lines after he went down. Flying to fire with Curt. I don't know how to be down here on the ground."

Again he reached out to brush a finger along the line still warm from her tears, but this time it was a caress.

"I love you, Maggie. That's what happened to me up there. It wasn't the damned tree. I figured out that I love you. Nothing in my life prepared me for the power of that realization. You share your bed with me, which is a gift I never imagined. But how can a lost cause like me ever give you what you want? What you deserve? Family? Children? Happy ever after? I can hear it in your voice. I can see it in the way you breathe. I can't give you that."

"Why not?" Maggie barely breathed the words. Had her mother ever loved her father as much as she loved this man? Impossible, or she'd never have left. She'd married a Coastie who loved his job as much as his family and been unable to live with that choice.

Palo just flapped his hands at himself, then let them fall by his side.

"I…" why were these things so hard to say? Maggie tried again. "I love you, too. I love Palo Akana."

He squinted at her. Because, like the good man he was, he'd never looked away.

"Yes, he pulled a crappy set of cards, but look at who he's become. And don't give me any *mierda* about genetic heritage. Whether they were teens in a gang or a drug-blasted whore, look at who you made, Palo. Palo is—*you are* an incredible man. And if you don't believe me, ask any one of the Firebirds."

"Don't think any of them are real happy with me at the moment."

"Feh!" Maggie waved that aside. "That's only because you almost killed them today. They'll get over it."

As if in answer, Drew and Amos rolled up in their black-and-flame GTOs. Stacy, Curt, Jana, Jasper, and Ty piled out as well.

"What are you all doing here?" Maggie knew from a month's experience that she needed peace and quiet to deal with Palo. She didn't need this!

"The way you tore outta there, Torres," Curt stuck his thumbs in his pockets and rocked back on his heels. "I figured Palo might need some backup."

"And them?" Maggie waved a hand at the others.

"We're talking Maggie Torres here. You don't think I'm dumb enough to take you on by myself." The others were grinning at her. Wasn't a man or woman in the outfit that didn't top her by at least six inches.

She considered reaching down and grabbing Palo's jack handle out of the dirt.

To hell with them all. She turned back to Palo.

"Well, looks like we get to do this in front of everyone." Maggie knew she was right and not even the collected Firebirds were going to stop her. "Are you spending the rest of your life with me? Or are you chickenshitting out because you had a crappy past? In which case, you can just keep right on driving."

Palo looked at her a long time, then glanced at all the cars pulled up around his. "Looks like I'm all parked in."

"Not good enough, Palo."

He grunted. "That's the challenge. Who's good enough for Maggie Torres?"

"C'mon, Palo." "Do it, Akana." The others were soon making so much noise that she knew there was no way for him to hear what she said, but she said it anyway, as one final plea.

"You are "

After a long pause—just looking her directly in the eyes —he nodded. Exactly like that time before he disappeared into the darkness around the campfire.

Maggie could feel her heart breaking.

But this time, he looked back up at her.

"You sure?" he mouthed silently.

Now it was her turn to nod—just like the *repeat after me* of a wedding.

He took a deep breath, then moved a single step forward and went down in front of her on one knee.

If the rabble of the Firebirds had been loud before, they exploded and Maggie could barely hear herself think.

So, when Palo reached out his hand, she took it and knelt before him.

"Together," she told him as the applause took over from the cheers.

Being a man of few words, he just pulled her into the safest place in the world and held her tight against his beautiful chest, just as she knew he would for all their days.

FIRE LIGHT, FIRE BRIGHT (EXCERPT)

IF YOU LIKED THIS, YOU'LL LOVE THE HOTSHOT SHORT STORIES!

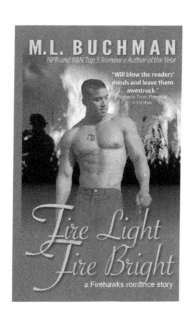

FIRE LIGHT, FIRE BRIGHT

(EXCERPT)

"Hi, I'm Candace Cantrell. First Rule: anyone who calls me Candy, who isn't my dad," she hooked a thumb at Fire Chief Carl Cantrell standing at-ease beside her, "is gonna get my boot up their ass. We clear on that?"

A rolling mumble of "Yes, ma'am." "Clear." and "Got it, Candace." rippled back to her from the recruits. Some answered almost as softly as the breeze working its way up through the tall pines. Others trumpeting it out as if to get her notice. A few offered simple nods.

She surveyed the line of recruits slowly. Way too early to make any judgments, but it was tempting. Day One, Minute One, and she could already guess five of the forty applicants weren't going to make it into the twenty slots she had open.

The one thing they all, including her dad, needed to see right up front was their team leader's complete confidence. Candace had been fighting wildfires for the U.S. Forest Service hotshot teams for a decade. She'd worked her way up to foreman twice, and had been gunning for a shot at superintendent of a whole twenty-person crew when her dad had called.

"We're got permission to form up an IHC in the heart of the Okanagan-Wenatchee National Forest," he never was long on greetings over the phone.

Her mouth had watered. A brand new Interagency Hotshot Crew didn't happen all that often.

"I talked to the other captains and we want you to form it up."

Now her throat had gone dry and she had to fight to not let it squeak.

"Me?"

"You aren't gonna let me down now, Candy Girl?"

"You shittin' me?" Not a chance.

Then he'd hit her with that big belly laugh of his.

"Knew you'd like the idea."

And simple as that, she'd been out of the San Juan IHC at the end of the Colorado fire season and back home in the Cascade Mountains of Washington State. She'd grown up in the resort town of Leavenworth—two thousand people and a ka-jillion tourists. The city fathers had transformed the failing timber town into a Bavarian wonderland back in the sixties. But that didn't stop the millions of acres of the National Forest and the rugged sagebrush-steppe ecosystem further east in central Washington from torching off every summer.

The very first thing she'd done, before she'd even left the San Juan IHC, was to call in a pair of ringers as her two foremen. Jess was short, feisty, and could walk up forested mountains all day with heavy gear without slowing down a bit. Patsy was tall, quiet, and tough. Candace had them stand in with the candidates for the first days because she wanted their eyes out there as well.

"Second, see that road?" she asked the recruits and

pointed to the foot of National Forest Road 6500. She'd had their first meet-up be here rather than at the fire hall in town. A gaggle of vehicles were pulled off the dirt of Little Wenatchee River Road. Beater pickups dominated, but there were a couple of hammered Civics, a pair of muscle cars, and a gorgeous Harley Davidson that she considered stealing it was so sweet.

The recruits all looked over their shoulders at the one lane of dirt.

"We're going for a stroll up that road. We leave in sixty seconds."

Like a herd of sheep, they all swung their heads to look at her.

"Fifty-five seconds, and this ain't gonna be a Sunday-type of a stroll."

You could tell the number of seasons they'd fought fire just by their reactions.

Five or more? They already wore their boots. Daypacks with water and energy bars were kept on their shoulders during her intro. And despite it being Day One of the ten-day shakedown, all had some tools: fold-up shovel and a heavy knife strapped to their leg at a minimum. Only she, Jess, and Patsy had Pulaski wildland fire axes tied to their gear, but all the veterans knew the drill.

Three to four seasons? Groans and eyerolls. Packs were on the ground beside them. No tools, but they knew what was coming now that she'd told them—ten kilometers, at least, and not one meter of it flat.

One to two seasons? Had the right boots on, but no packs. They were racing back to their vehicles to see what equipment they could assemble.

Rookies? Tennis shoes, ball caps, no gear, blank stares.

"Forty-five seconds, rooks. Boots and water. If you're

not on the trail in fifty seconds, you're off the crew." That got their asses moving.

There was one man on the whole crew she couldn't pigeonhole, the big guy who'd climbed off the Harley. His pack and the fold-up shovel strapped to it were so new they sparkled. But his boots and the massive hunting knife on his thigh both showed very heavy use.

A glance at her Dad's assessing gaze confirmed it. Something was odd about the Harley man and his easy grin. Not rugged handsome, but still very nice to look at. Powerful shoulders, slim waist. Not an athlete's build, but rather someone who really used his body. His worn jeans revealed that he already had the powerful legs that every hotshot would develop from endless miles of chasing fire over these mountains and steppes for the next six months. It was like he was a Hollywood movie: some parts of him were so very right, but a lot of the details were dead wrong.

***

Luke Rawlings looked at the team superintendent. Couldn't help himself, 'cause damn she was a treat to look at. Her white-blond hair was short and sassy, her body was seriously fit, but curved like a sweet-Candy dream girl. Her no-nonsense attitude just cracked him up; he could hear that natural state of command that you only learned the hard way, by doing it. Not something he'd ever expected to find in a hot civilian babe.

When he'd mustered out, SEAL Lieutenant Commander Altman had suggested he try firefighting. Altman was a smart dude, so Luke had followed his suggestion. He'd kicked around with a big city fire department doing ride-alongs for a while. Chicago Fire were all super guys and they kept trying to sign him aboard, but tramping pavement and cement, doing fire inspections for date tags on commercial fire extinguishers…he'd rather be back in the African jungle. If his nerves would let him, which he so wasn't going to think about now.

He still wasn't sure how he'd heard about the hotshot crews, but walking into a wildfire—he just liked the way it sounded.

And looking at "Not Candy" Cantrell, he was damn glad he'd followed his whim and ridden his Harley west.

Available at fine retailers everywhere!
Fire Light, Fire Bright

ABOUT THE AUTHOR

M.L. Buchman started the first of, what is now over 50 novels and as many short stories, while flying from South Korea to ride his bicycle across the Australian Outback. Part of a solo around the world trip that ultimately launched his writing career.

All three of his military romantic suspense series—The Night Stalkers, Firehawks, and Delta Force— have had a title named "Top 10 Romance of the Year" by the American Library Association's *Booklist*. NPR and Barnes & Noble have named other titles "Top 5 Romance of the Year." In 2016 he was a finalist for Romance Writers of America prestigious RITA award. He also writes: contemporary romance, thrillers, and fantasy.

Past lives include: years as a project manager, rebuilding and single-handing a fifty-foot sailboat, both flying and jumping out of airplanes, and he has designed and built two houses. He is now making his living as a full-time writer on the Oregon Coast with his beloved wife and is constantly amazed at what you can do with a degree in Geophysics. You may keep up with his writing and receive a free starter e-library by subscribing to his newsletter at: www.mlbuchman.com

Join the conversation:
www.mlbuchman.com

Other works by M. L. Buchman:

SIGN UP FOR M. L. BUCHMAN'S
NEWSLETTER TODAY

and receive:
Release News
Free Short Stories
a Free Book

Do it today. Do it now.
http://free-book.mlbuchman.com

81711164R00050

Made in the USA
Lexington, KY
21 February 2018